2009

Dear Friends,

40 years ago THE VERY HUNGRY CATERPILLAR was published. I am often asked where did the idea for this book come from. Well, one day, with a hole-puncher, I playfully punched some holes into a stack of papers. Looking at the holes I thought of a bookworm. Then I changed the bookworm into a green worm. With the help of my good editor Ann Beneduce, the green worm became a caterpillar. That was the beginning...

Since then millions of children, speaking many languages, have enjoyed this book all over the world.

To you all THE VERY HUNGRY CATERPILLAR and I send our

BEST WISHES

Eric Carle

THE VERY HUNGRY CATERPILLAR

by Eric Carle

PHILOMEL BOOKS

ALSO BY ERIC CARLE

The Very Busy Spider
The Very Quiet Cricket
The Very Lonely Firefly
The Very Clumsy Click Beetle
1, 2, 3 to the Zoo
Animals Animals
Dragons Dragons
Draw Me a Star
Dream Snow
The Honeybee and the Robber
Little Cloud
Mister Seahorse
"Slowly, Slowly, Slowly," Said the Sloth
Today Is Monday

Copyright © 1969 and 1987 by Eric Carle.
Published by Philomel Books, a division of Penguin Young Readers Group,
345 Hudson Street, New York, NY 10014.
First Published in 1969 by The World Publishing Company,
Cleveland and New York. All rights reserved.
No part of this book may be reproduced in any form without written permission
from the publisher, except for brief passages included in a review. Manufactured in China.
Eric Carle's name and logotype are registered trademarks of Eric Carle.

Library of Congress Cataloging-in-Publication Data
Carle, Eric. The very hungry caterpillar.
Summary: Follows the progress of a very hungry caterpillar as he eats his way through
varied and very large quantity of food, until, full at last, he forms a cocoon around
himself and goes to sleep. [1. Caterpillars-Fiction.] I. Title. PZ7.C2147Ve [E] 79-13202
ISBN 978-0-399-25556-4
10 9 8 7 6 5 4 3 2 1

7-81375-21819-0
Kohls
14-421819-12
123386
09/10-02/11

This special edition was printed for Kohl's Department Stores, Inc.
(for distribution on behalf of Kohl's Cares, LLC, its wholly owned subsidiary)
by Philomel Books, a division of Penguin Young Readers Group, New York.

For my sister Christa

In the light of the moon
a little egg lay on a leaf.

One Sunday morning the warm sun came up and—pop!—out of the egg came a tiny and very hungry caterpillar.

He started to look for some food.

On Friday
he ate through
five oranges,
but he was still
hungry.

On Saturday
he ate through
one piece of
chocolate cake, one ice-cream cone, one pickle, one slice of Swiss cheese, one slice of salami,

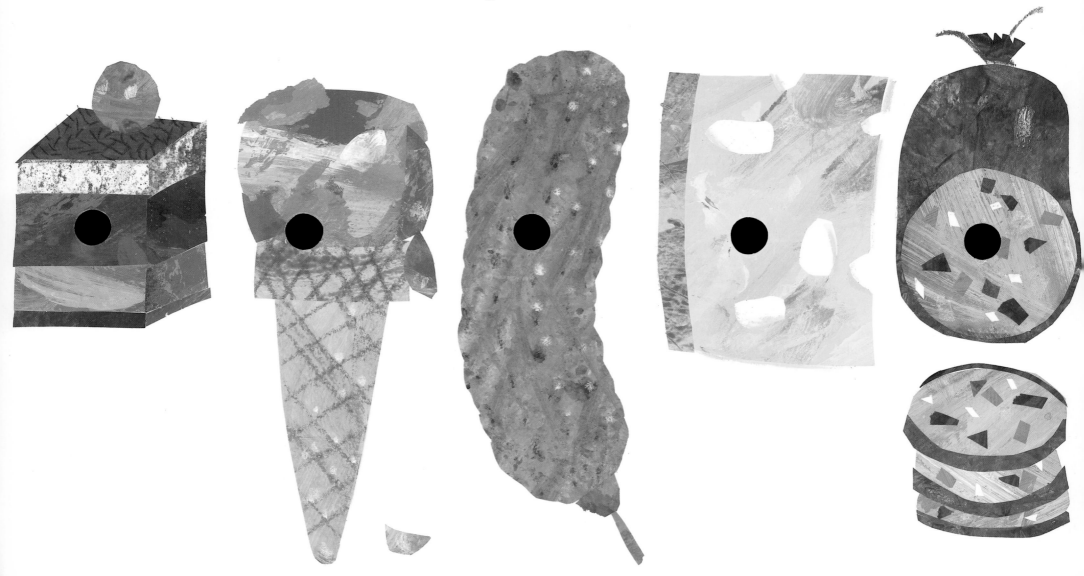

one lollipop, one piece of cherry pie, one sausage, one cupcake, and one slice of watermelon.

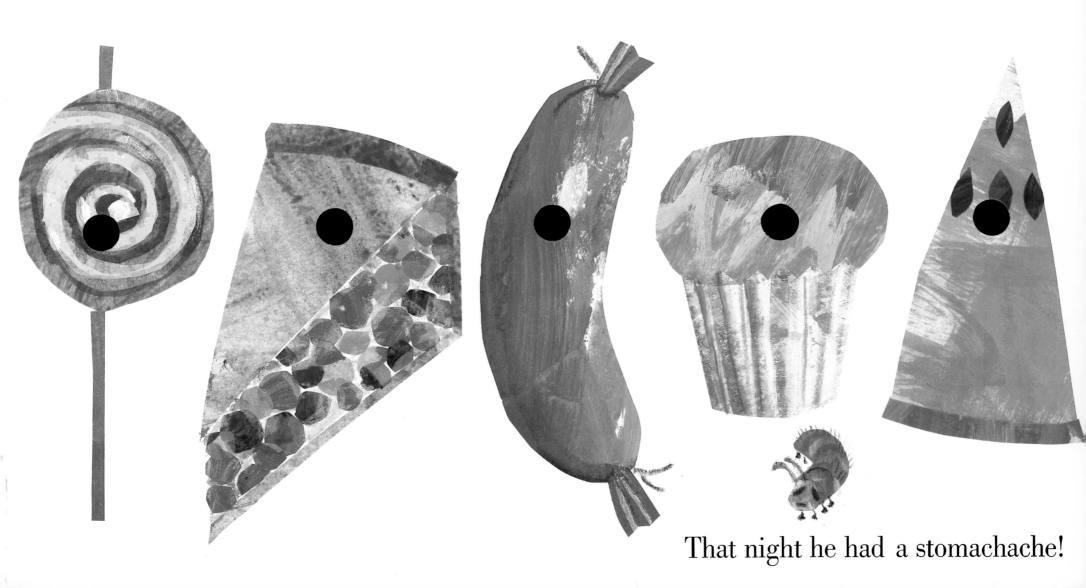

That night he had a stomachache!

The next day was Sunday again.
The caterpillar ate through
one nice green leaf,
and after that he felt
much better.

Now he wasn't hungry any more—and he wasn't a little caterpillar any more.
He was a big, fat caterpillar.

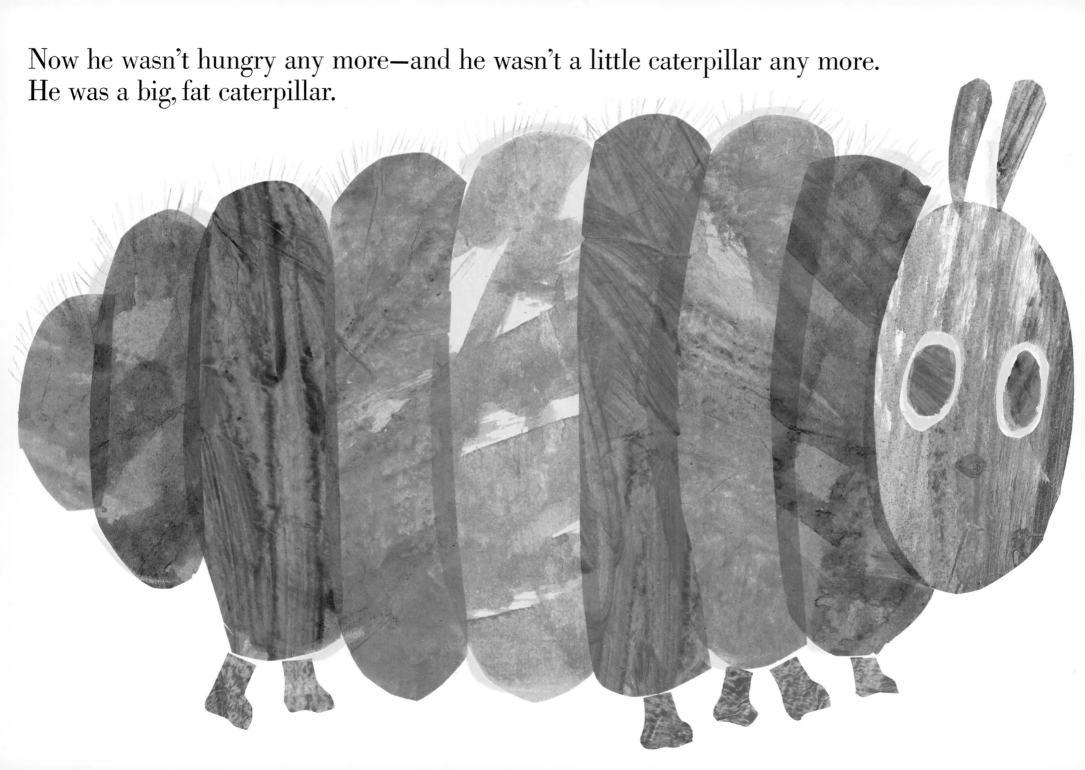

He built a small house, called a cocoon, around himself. He stayed inside for more than two weeks. Then he nibbled a hole in the cocoon, pushed his way out and . . .

he was a beautiful butterfly!